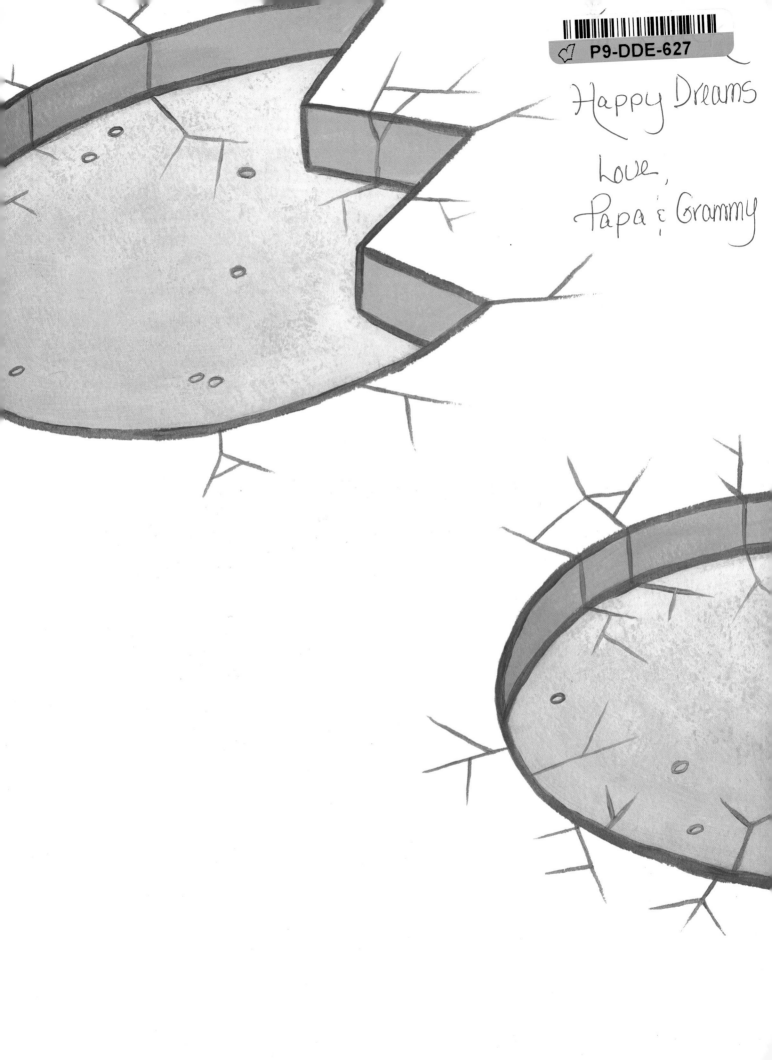

P9-DDE-627

Happy Dreams

Love,
Papa & Grammy

For Max, my consultant paleontologist—J. E.

For Andrew, my beautiful boy—C. J.

Text copyright 2001 by Jonathan Emmett
Illustrations copyright 2001 by Curtis Jobling
First published in Great Britain in 2001 by HarperCollins Publishers Ltd.
All rights reserved.
Printed in Singapore.
No part of this book may be reproduced or copied in any form
without written permission from the publisher.
GOLDEN BOOKS®, A GOLDEN BOOK®, and G DESIGN®
are registered trademarks of Golden Books Publishing Company, Inc.
The distinctive spine is a trademark of Golden Books Publishing Company, Inc.
10 9 8 7 6 5 4 3 2 1

Library of Congress Cataloging-in-Publication Data
Emmett, Jonathan.
Dinosaurs after dark / Jonathan Emmett ; illustrated by Curtis Jobling.
p. cm.
Summary: Sleepless Bobby hears noise outside his bedroom window,
and when he follows it into the city he finds some dinosaurs to play with.
ISBN 0-307-41179-6 (alk. paper)
[1. Night—Fiction. 2. Dinosaurs—Fiction.] I. Jobling, Curtis, ill. II. Title.
PZ7.E696 Di 2001   [E]—dc21   2001040447

DINOSAURS AFTER DARK

Jonathan Emmett
& Curtis Jobling

 A Golden Book ◆ New York

Golden Books Publishing Company, Inc., New York, New York 10106

This is the story of Bobby, who was lonely in the night.

And how, when everyone else was sleeping, he heard the sound of something sneaking softly past his window.

And how he crept across the floor,

and took a peep outside and saw . . .

a huge enormous

So Bobby grabbed his robe

and left his room   and tiptoed down the stairs

and through the hall,   out of the house into the city.

The monster crept from street to street,
and Bobby followed after it,

past unlit shops and office blocks,
and dark, deserted buildings.

Until they reached the city square,

But when they saw Bobby, they roared
and ran after him, chanting:

"Snatch him!"

"Munch him!"   "Catch him!"

"Crunch him!"

"Before he runs
and tells on us!"

But Bobby promised not to tell,
and crossed it on his heart as well.

And so, instead of eating him, they let him join the fun:

sliding down the rooftops above the city hall,

climbing up the office blocks, then jumping off them all.

Splashing in the fountains and swinging from the cranes,

racing through the station and playing with the trains.

Underground and in the air,
those dinosaurs played everywhere!

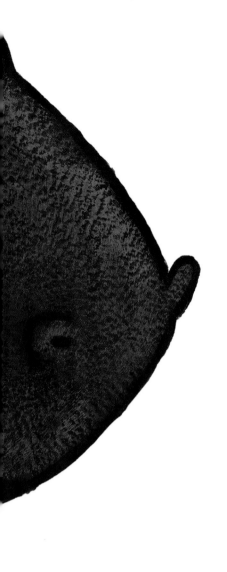

"Now for one last game," they cried,
"of hide-and-seek, and you can hide."

"Yes, you can hide,
and we will seek you,

but if we find you,

we might

eat

you!"

So Bobby ran and ran and ran, until he found somewhere snug and safe and secret, where nobody would find him!

And he curled up small and held his breath and listened for the sound of the dinosaurs' feet.

But all he heard was his own heart thumping, slower and slower and slower ...

until he fell fast asleep.

Then, someone did find him, and picked him up,
and carried him through the night, back to his bed,
where he sighed and smiled and slept . . .

. . . until morning.

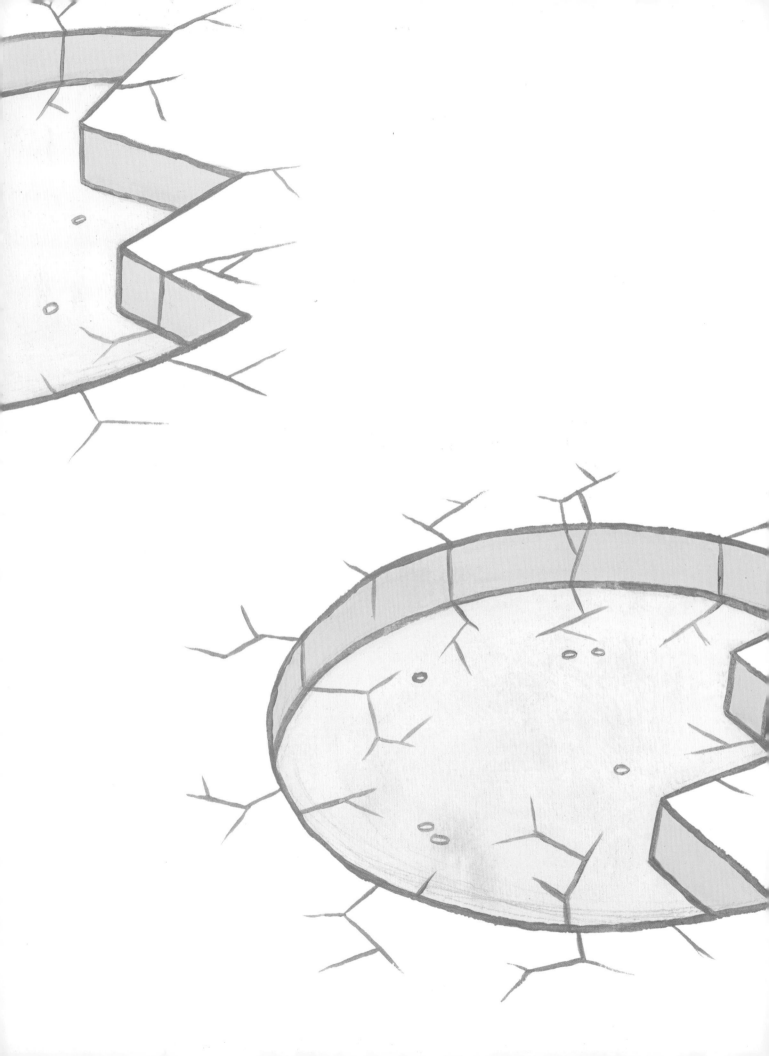